Backyard Cricket

Written by Anne Garton
Illustrated by Leigh Brown

www.childrensebooks.com.au

We're standing in the shade of the Mango tree,

Davo, Bob, Jacko, Tom and me.

The backyard's the pitch. A garbage bin's the wicket.

In the stinking summer heat, we're playing backyard cricket...

Underneath the Mango tree.

Jacko's fielding where the sun meets the shade.

We're using a bat that my Dad made.

Davo's at the crease. Tom's in the keeper's gloves.

My sister Jenny pegs washing, but it's cricket she loves...

Underneath the Mango tree.

Bob's running in and bowling like Shane Warne.

Davo hits a six across the lawn.

He drives it to the fence, but Bluey nicks the ball.

We grab the thieving dog and it's an all in brawl...

Underneath the Mango tree.

Tom's crouching at the wicket. He taps the bin.

That's the signal he's ready. Bob runs in.

Davo tips the ball and it sails right through the back.

It hits Tom in the nose with a stinging smack...

Underneath the Mango tree.

Davo hits as Jenny pegs sheets on the line.

The ball hits the covers. She catches it in time.

Jenny's caught the ball so it's her turn to bat.

The boys whine, 'That's not fair, we don't like that!'

Underneath the Mango tree.

Jenny's batting at the crease all dressed in pink.

She won't hit the ball, so we think.

She whacks it to the street. We are so surprised.

We make her lose her turn, so she just stands and cries...

Underneath the Mango tree.

Tom's standing at the wicket ready to bat.

He can't see a thing with his great big hat.

He swings and hits the dustbin, so we all yell, 'HOWZAT?'

He refuses to move until he has another bat...

Underneath the Mango tree.

Jacko's squatting half-asleep, just at slips.

He misses a catch, stumbles and trips.

The ball sails right into Mum's veggie patch.

We trample all her strawberries trying to get it back...

Underneath the Mango tree.

Mum's bringing out some icy poles. What a treat!

It's time to take a break, in the sticky heat.

We lie on the grass looking up at the sky.

We listen to Bluey trying to bite the flies...

Underneath the Mango tree.

The afternoon is fading. The cicadas start to drone.

Tom jumps the fence—time for home.

Jenny drops an icy pole as she's about to lick it.

She storms off and crashes through the dustbin wicket...

Underneath the Mango tree.

The sun's slowly setting and it will be dark soon.

The ball gets lost in the twilight gloom.

We've all had fun and played our very best.

We'll be back tomorrow for the second test...

In the stinking summer heat we're playing backyard cricket...

Safe and sound beneath the Mango tree.

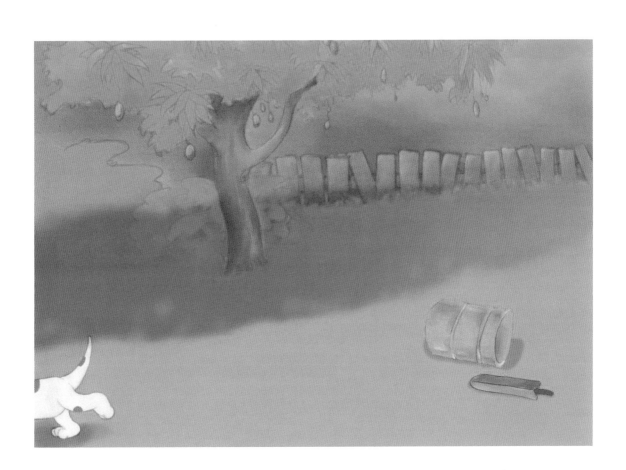

Acknowledgments

Published in 2008 in Australia by
CHILDREN'S EBOOKS PTY LTD
GPO Box 178 Wilston 4051
© Anne Garton 2008
Edition 3
Illustrated by: Leigh Brown
ISBN: 978-0-9804820-6-5
Editor: Jennifer Voss
www.childrensebooks.com.au

Other CHILDREN'S EBOOKS
A day out at Phillip Island
Days go by
Gypsy and Hotham
Little Em
My Teacher is a Witch
My Queensland
Mr Nobody's here
Patchy Scratchy
Someone left the gate open at the Zoo!
The Bicycle
The Bully
The Footballer
The Spider in the Christmas tree
The Tooth Fairy
The Wetlands
This Precious Day

Visit the website and preview all these eBooks:
www.childrensebooks.com.au

Made in the USA
Lexington, KY
25 August 2011